WATER, WATER

by Eloise Greenfield
pictures by Jan Spivey Gilchrist

HarperFestival®
A Division of HarperCollinsPublishers

Water in my fishbowl,

water on my face,

rainwater falling all over the place.

I see rivers and streams,

oceans and seas,

cool, cool water
splashing over
my knees.

I see lakes and ponds

and waterfalls, oh,

water, water, water, everywhere I go.

Water in the fountain,

water in the sink. . . .

May I please have a little water to drink?

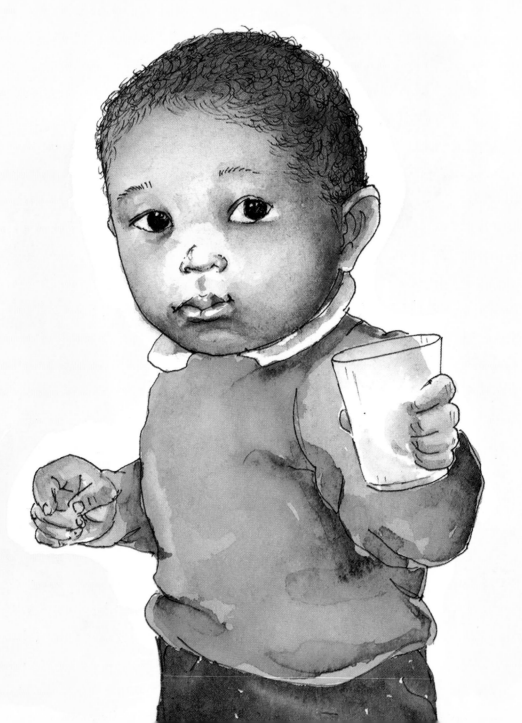

Good, good water in my cup,

I drink it *all* up!